S0-CBW-419

Beginner Biography

Elizabeth Cady Stanton

Fighter for Women's Rights

by Jeri Cipriano
illustrated by Scott R. Brooks

Red Chair Press Egremont, Massachusetts

Look! Books are produced and published by Red Chair Press:
Red Chair Press LLC PO Box 333 South Egremont, MA 01258-0333
www.redchairpress.com

 FREE lesson guide at www.redchairpress.com/free-activities

Publisher's Cataloging-In-Publication Data
Names: Cipriano, Jeri S., author. | Brooks, Scott R., 1963- illustrator.

Title: Elizabeth Cady Stanton: fighter for women's rights / by Jeri Cipriano; illustrated by Scott R. Brooks.

Description: Egremont, Massachusetts : Red Chair Press, [2020] | Series: Look! books. Beginner biography | Includes index and resources for further reading. | Interest age level: 005-008. | Summary: "When Elizabeth Cady Stanton was a young girl, she knew she could do anything her brothers could do. But the laws in the country said women were not equal to men. Elizabeth knew she had to make a difference for all women."--Provided by publisher.

Identifiers: ISBN 9781634409872 (library hardcover) | ISBN 9781634409889 (paperback) | ISBN 9781634409896 (ebook)

Subjects: LCSH: Stanton, Elizabeth Cady, 1815-1902--Juvenile literature. | Feminists--United States--Biography--Juvenile literature. | Women's rights--United States--History--19th century--Juvenile literature. | CYAC: Stanton, Elizabeth Cady, 1815-1902. | Feminists--United States--Biography. | Women's rights--United States--History--19th century.

Classification: LCC HQ1413.S67 C35 2020 (print) | LCC HQ1413.S67 (ebook) | DDC 305.42/092 B--dc23

Library of Congress Control Number: 2019938726

Photo credits: Library Of Congress: 14, 19, 21; Shutterstock: 20

Printed in the United States of America

0819 1P CGS20

Table of Contents

A Girl is Born

On November 12, 1815, Elizabeth Cady was born. Growing up, she would have fewer chances in life than her brothers.

Girls could not go to boys' colleges. They could not have their own money or property. They could not vote.

Elizabeth was born a fighter. She would fight all her life for what she thought was right.

The Girl Grows Up

Elizabeth liked to visit her father at work. She went to his law office often. There, she learned that women had very few rights under the law.

Men had all the jobs. Men passed all the laws. Women had no say at all.

This made Elizabeth angry.

When it was time for college, Elizabeth went to a woman's college. It was different from men's colleges. It **prepared** women to raise children and care for their homes. Men's colleges prepared them for jobs.

After college, Elizabeth liked visiting her cousin Libby. Libby's home was always filled with people.

Men *and* women spoke about ending slavery. They wanted to make the world a better place.

Marriage

When Elizabeth was 24 years old, she met Henry Stanton. He liked how Elizabeth was not shy. She let people know what she thought.

The next year, in 1840, they married. Elizabeth surprised everyone. She did not say she would "obey" her husband. She felt they were equals.

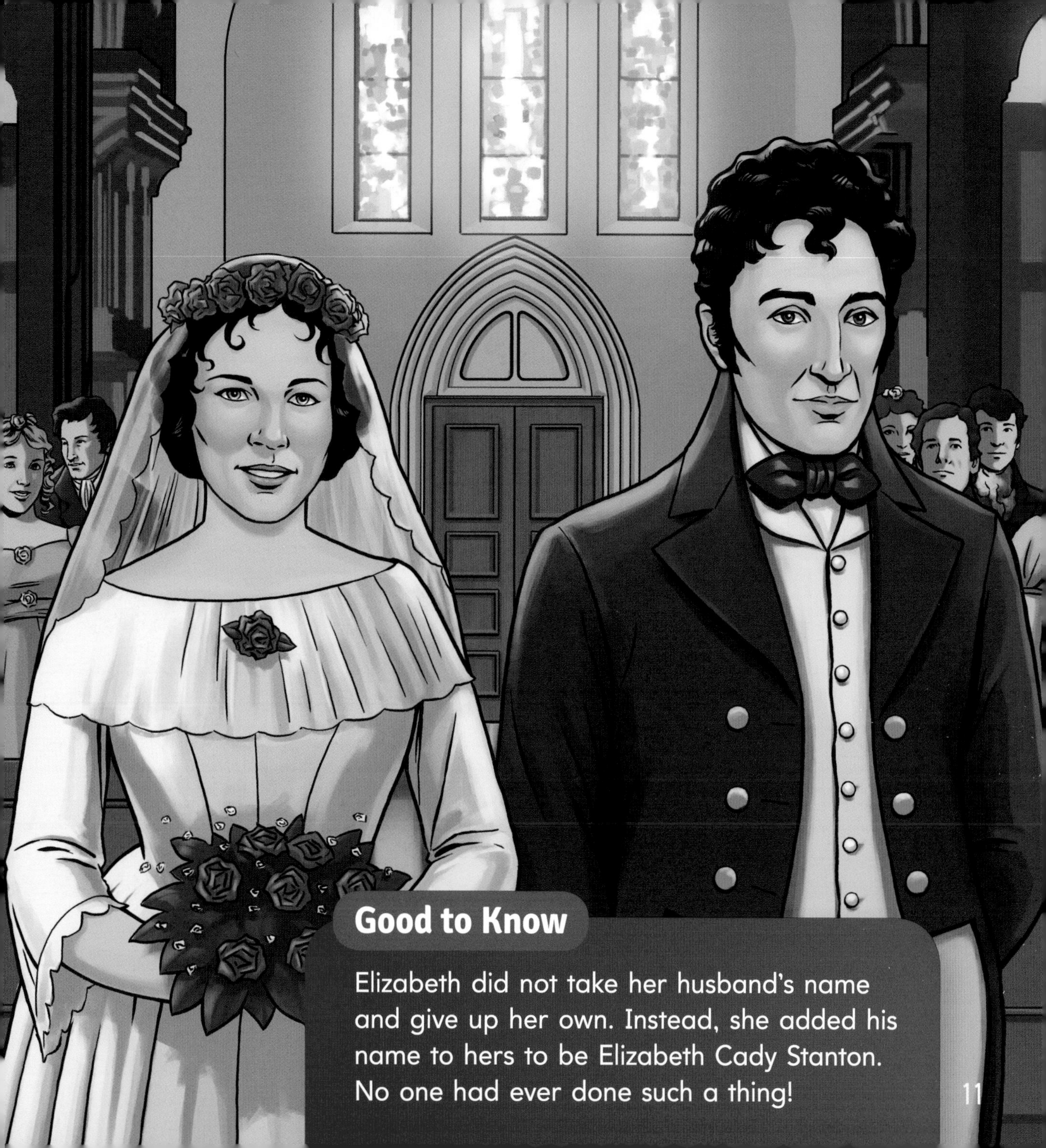

Good to Know

Elizabeth did not take her husband's name and give up her own. Instead, she added his name to hers to be Elizabeth Cady Stanton. No one had ever done such a thing!

Making New Friends

Henry and Elizabeth traveled to London, England for a big meeting. There, Henry spoke out against slavery.

At the meeting, women were not allowed to speak. They had to sit apart from men. Elizabeth was angry. In London, she met Lucretia (loo-cree-sha) Mott who felt the same. The two became friends.

Lucretia Mott would become a fighter for women's rights—just like Elizabeth.

In 1847, Elizabeth's family moved to Seneca Falls, New York. By then, she had three children. (She would have seven children in all.)

Elizabeth and her daughter, 1856

One day, Lucretia Mott invited Elizabeth to meet some friends. Elizabeth met women who thought it was time to fight for women's rights.

Women's Rights

A big meeting was planned for July 1848. An ad in the newspaper invited people to "discuss the condition and rights of women."

Elizabeth wrote a new version of the **Declaration** of Independence. In it, she wrote "all men and women are created equal."

She read her declaration at the meeting. Then 100 people signed it—68 women and 32 men.

Partners

In 1851, Elizabeth met Susan B. Anthony, another leader for women's rights. Working together, they led the women's **movement**.

Success! In 1860, New York passed new laws. Now women could have their own money. Now women had more rights under the law. But women were still not equal to men.

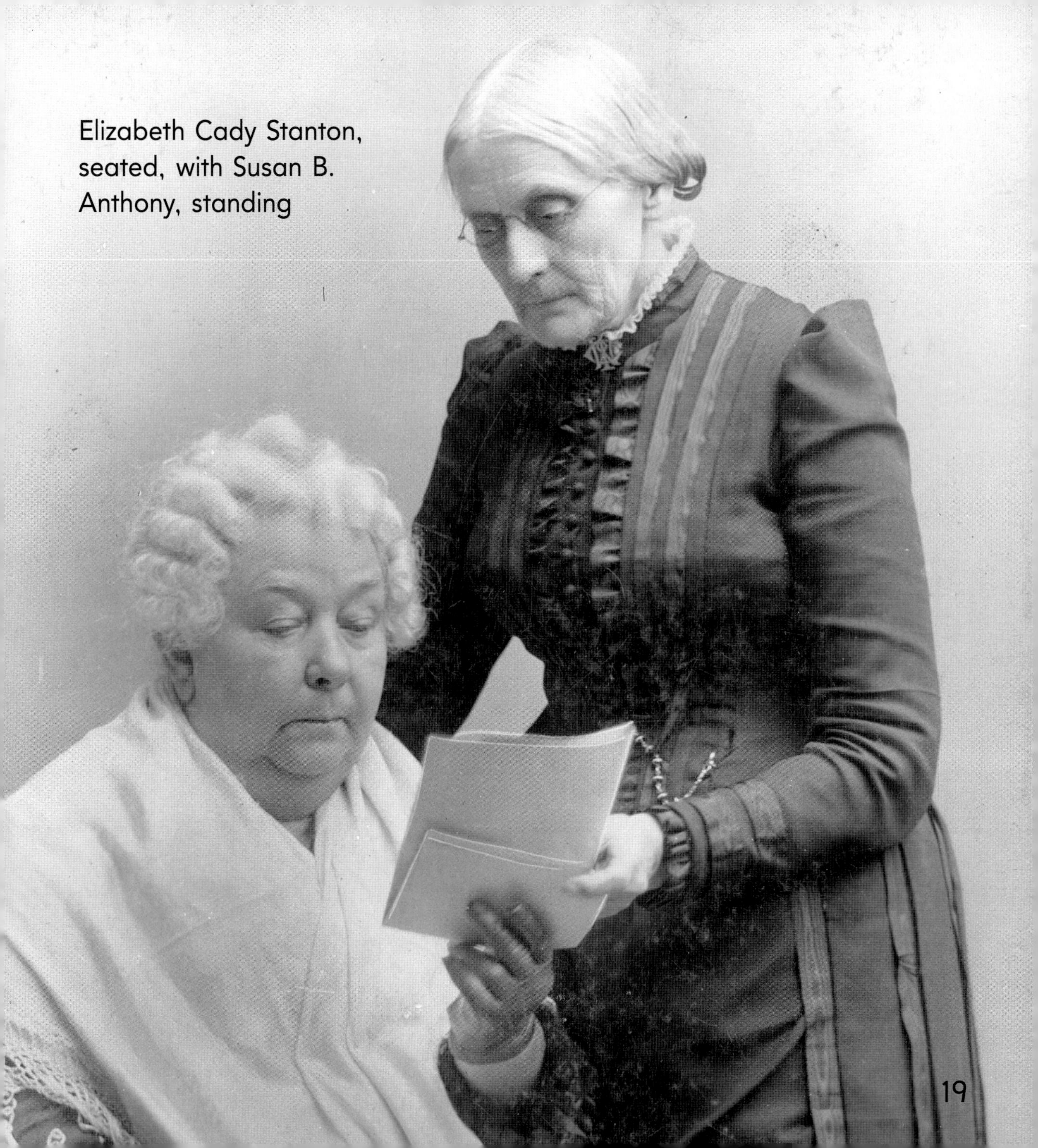

Elizabeth Cady Stanton, seated, with Susan B. Anthony, standing

The Fight to Vote

In 1872, Stanton and Anthony asked lawmakers for an **amendment** that would give women the right to vote.

That amendment went to Congress in 1878. It did not get enough votes to pass—not that year or for many years after.

This monument in Seneca Falls, NY, shows Stanton, Elizabeth Bloomer, and Anthony.

The Right to Vote

Elizabeth died in 1902 at age 87. The fight she helped start in 1848 went on. Finally, 72 years later, in 1920, women had the right to vote across the country.

Timeline: Big Dates in Stanton's Life

1815: Elizabeth is born in Johnstown, New York.

1832: She graduates from Troy Female Seminary.

1840: Elizabeth Cady marries Henry Stanton.

1847: The family moves to Seneca Falls, New York.

1851: She begins working with Susan B. Anthony for women's rights.

1860: New York passes laws to give women more rights.

1861: U.S. Civil War begins.

1862: She moves to New York City and continues to fight against slavery and for women's rights.

1865: The Civil War ends.

1902: Elizabeth dies.

1920: Women vote for the first time everywhere in the U.S.

Good to Know

People vote to make changes in how they live. What changes would you vote for if you could vote today?

Words to Know

amendment a change that is added to the United States Constitution, the written laws of the land.

declaration a statement or announcement

movement people working together to bring about a change

prepared to be ready for something

Learn More at the Library

(Check out these books to read with others.)

Rappaport, Doreen. *Elizabeth Started All the Trouble.* Disney-Hyperion, 2016.

Stone, Tanya Lee. *Elizabeth Leads the Way: Elizabeth Cady Stanton and the Right to Vote,* Square Fish, 2010.

Mead, Maggie. *Suffrage Sisters, The Fight for Liberty.* Red Chair Press, 2015.

Index

About the Author

Jeri Cipriano has written more than a hundred books for young readers. She enjoys reading and finding out new things. She likes to share what she learns. And, she votes at home in New York State.